A gift from the
Home and School Club
1985-86

DATE DUE

FEB 2 4 1988			
APR 0 6 1989			
JUN 1 1988			
FEB 0 7 1989			
FEB 2 7 1989			
MAR 0 8 1989			
MAR 2 2 1989			
MAY 2 3 1989			
OCT 0 2 1989	1989		
Oct 2 0			
MAY 1 7 1990			

STORY AND
PICTURES
BY
IVAN
GANTSCHEV

THE VOL-CANO

NEUGEBAUER PRESS, LONDON

Far out to sea, a long long way from here,
there is a beautiful island.

On the island there are lots of colourful trees
and many kinds of animals.

There is a huge waterfall, and even a volcano
that spits out fire and rocks every now and then.

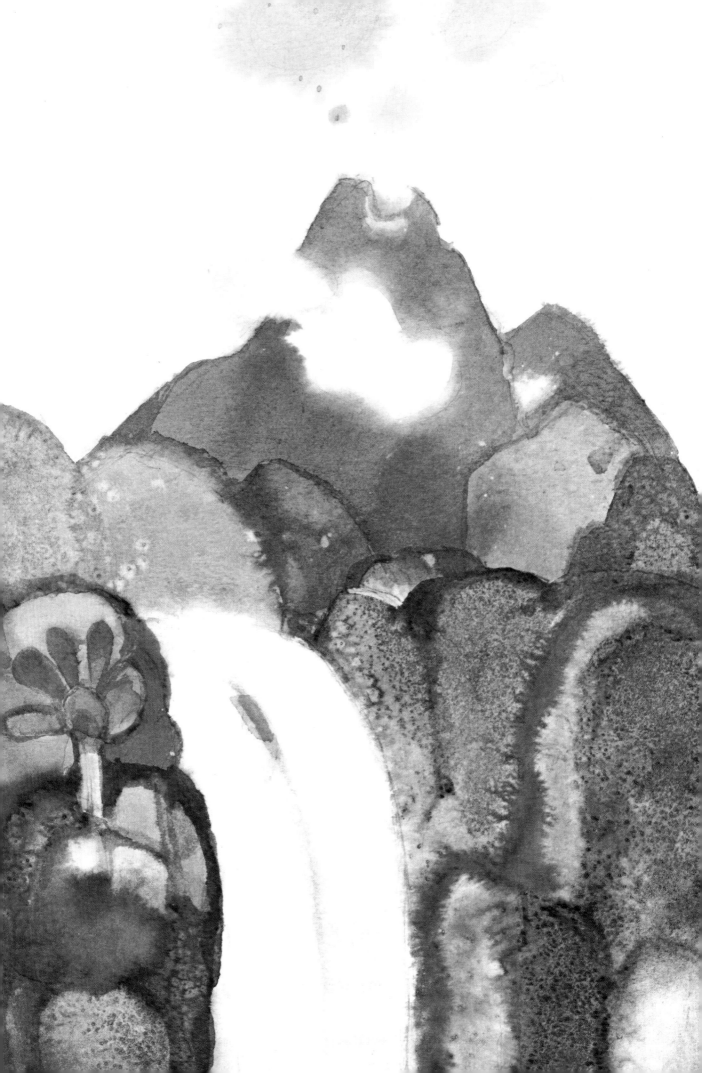

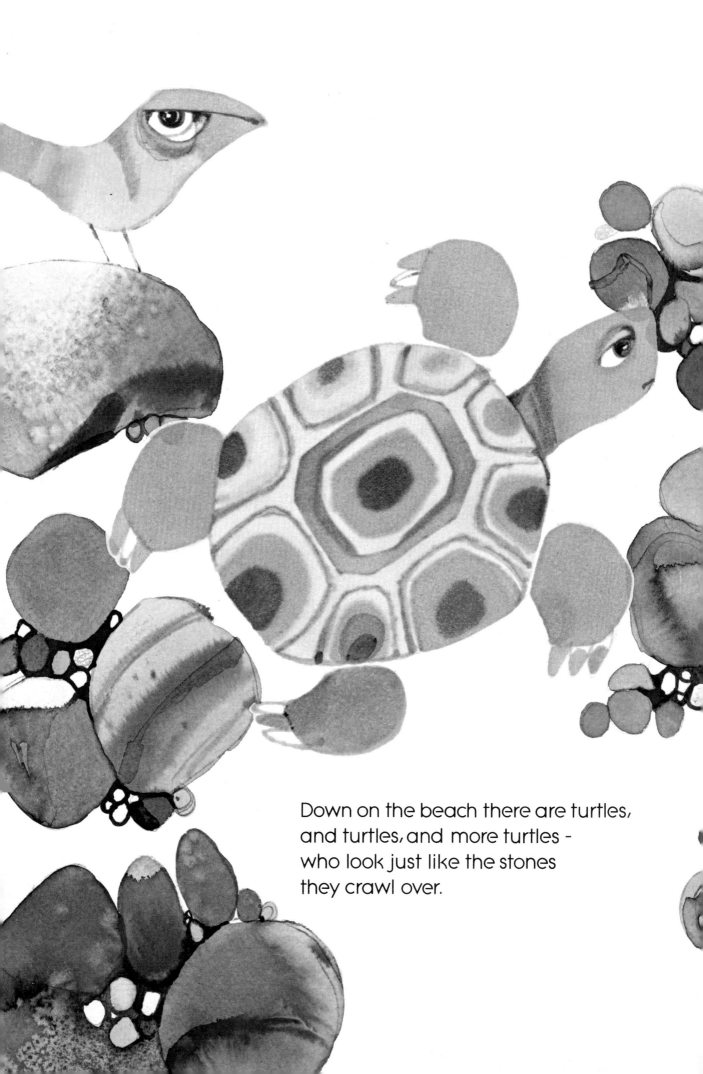

Down on the beach there are turtles,
and turtles, and more turtles -
who look just like the stones
they crawl over.

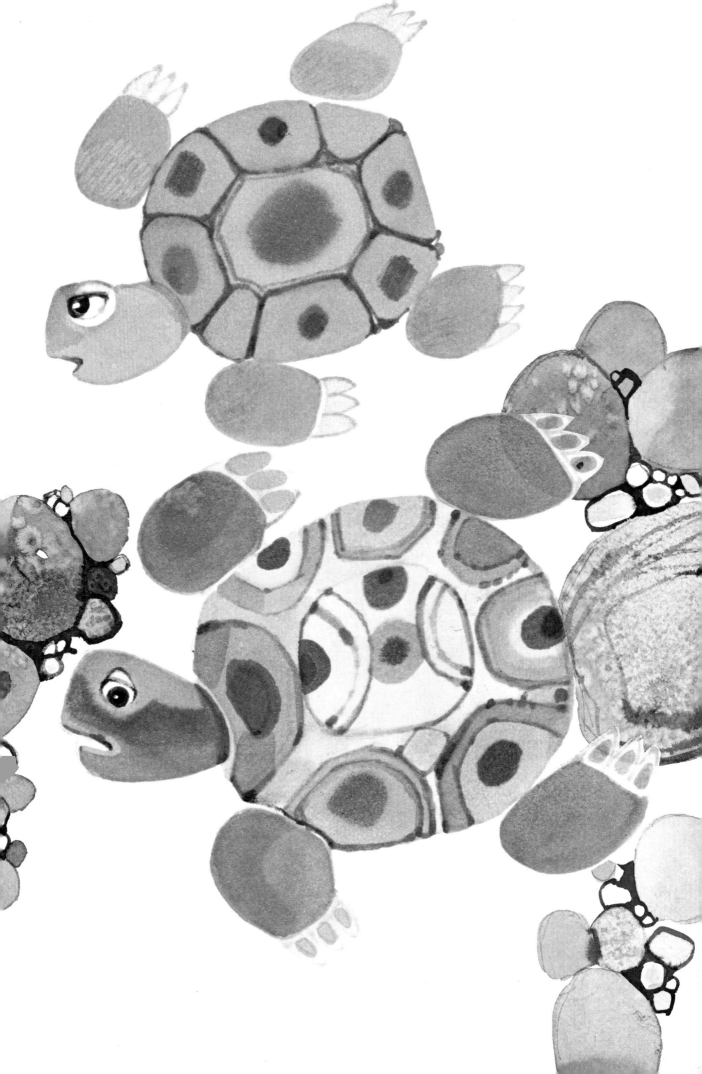

Now for as long as anyone can remember
everything has been calm and peaceful
on the island. But it wasn't always so.
Once, long long ago
there was a great upheaval.
It was all the fault of Brok,
the evil giant crab
who lived under the waterfall.

Brok hated everything
on the island,
but most of all
he hated the volcano.

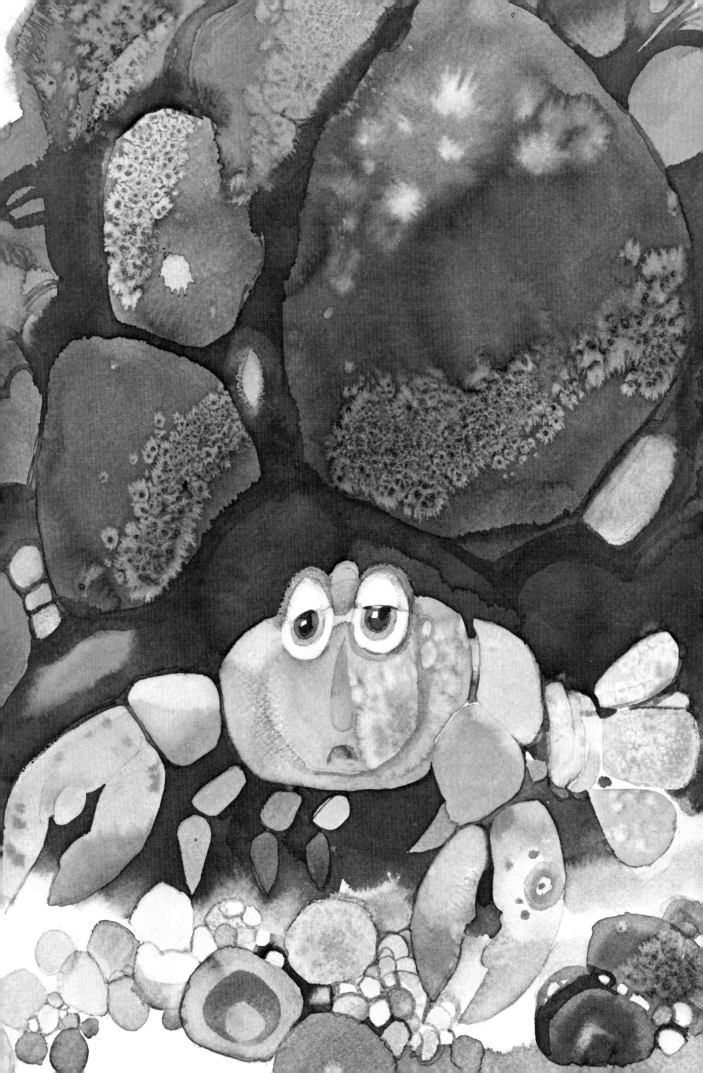

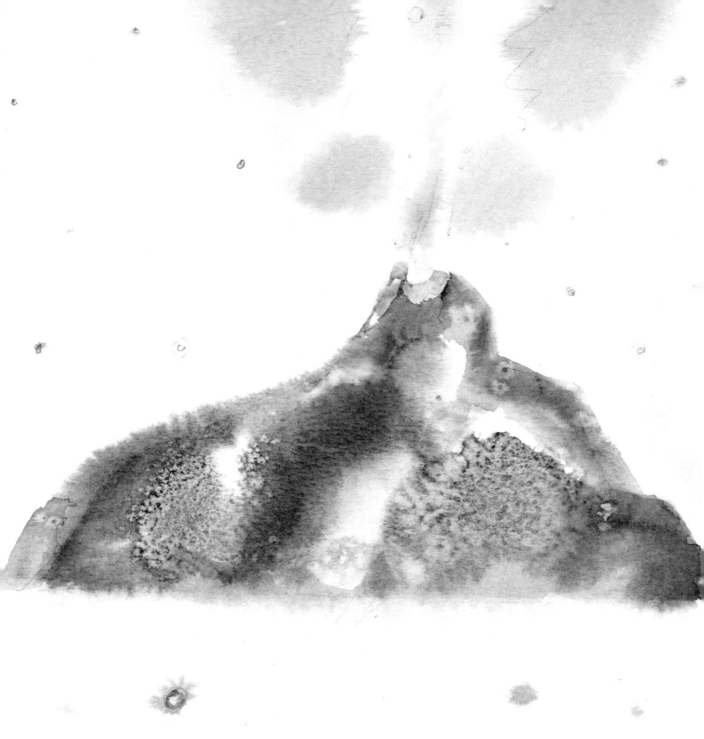

And so Brok persuaded the river to drill down
into the volcano and put out the fire at its heart.

After many years of wearing away the rocks,
the water finally reached the fiery centre of the volcano.

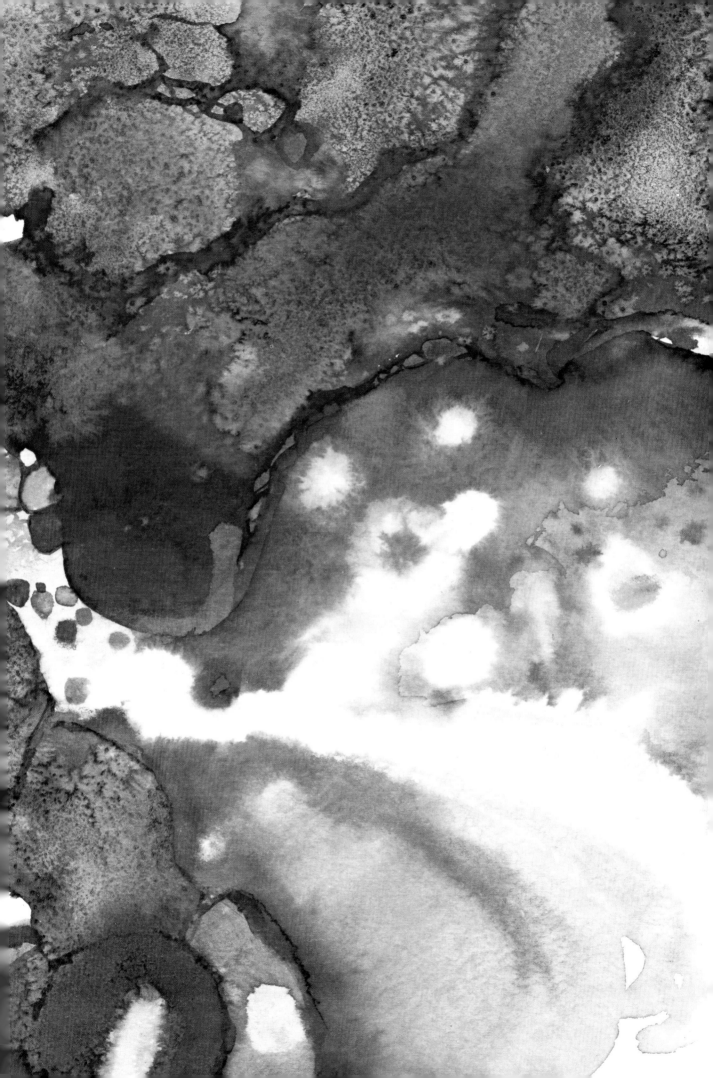

But the water could not put out the fire.
Instead, the volcano exploded
with a terrible crash.

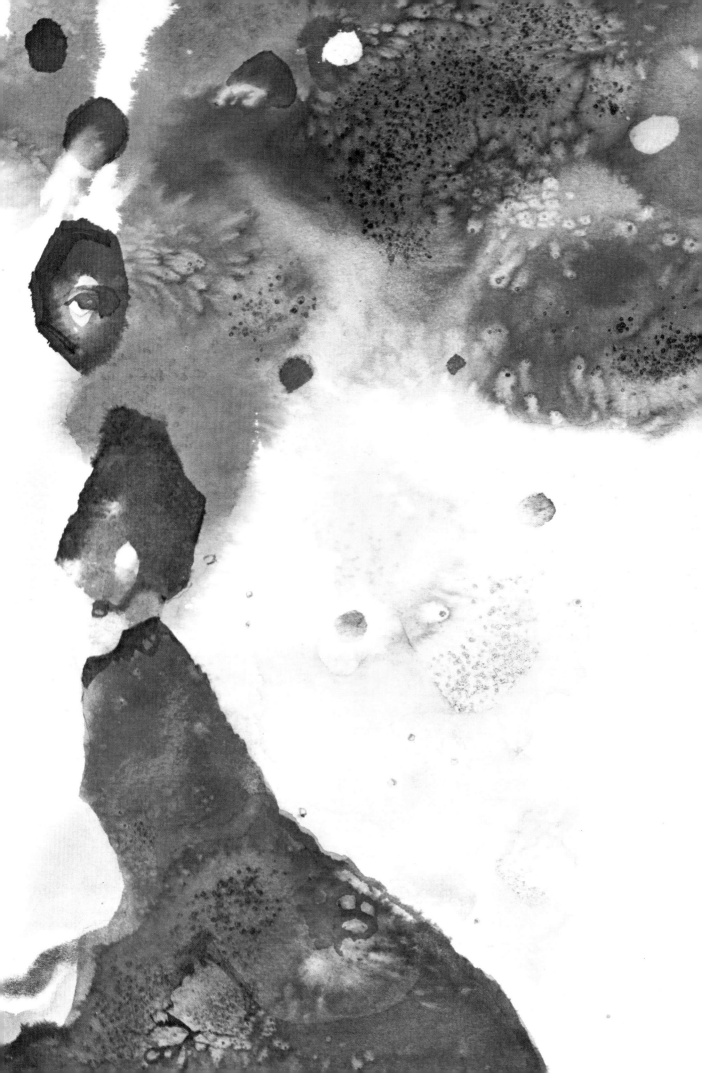

The whole island
was smashed to pieces,
and even Brok was sent
flying through the air.

At last when everything had calmed down, the animals
saw that the island had changed completely.
Below the waterfall, there was now a beautiful lake,
where the pelicans could fish in peace.

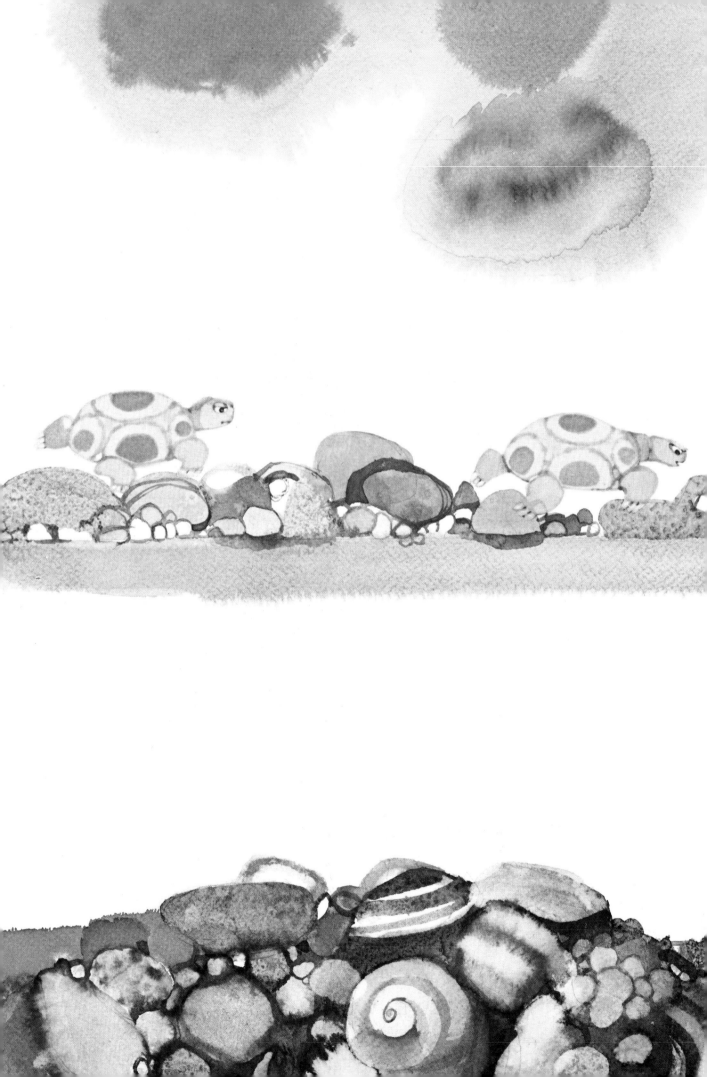

The volcano too was quiet, and the turtles admired its
reflection in the lake as they crawled slowly amongst the stones.
But what had happened to Brok?

Brok the trouble-maker had been thrown by the volcano onto the top of a tall tree.
A bird took the crab from the tree, thinking he'd make a good supper. But Brok smelt so horrible that the bird dropped him instead somewhere in the sea, and no-one has seen him from that day to this.

And that is the story of the volcano as I heard it.
I'd like to go to that island one day, and see the beautiful lake
with its pelicans, and the mountain that was once a volcano.
I'd try to imagine how the island used to be,
with the volcano spitting out fire and rocks.
But I'd be glad enough not to meet Brok, the giant crab!

Whenever I hear of some other volcano, in another country,
that has erupted, I wonder whether perhaps Brok was
washed up on that shore, and started his trouble-making
all over again.

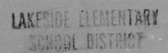